DRACULA'S CAT

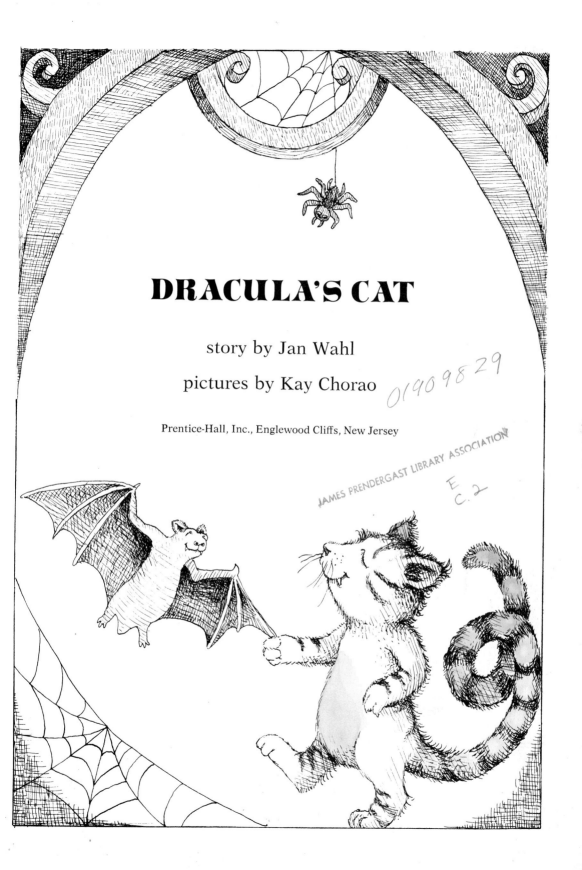

DRACULA'S CAT

story by Jan Wahl

pictures by Kay Chorao

Prentice-Hall, Inc., Englewood Cliffs, New Jersey

Printed in the United States of America

Prentice-Hall International, Inc., London
Prentice-Hall of Australia, Pty. Ltd., North Sydney
Prentice-Hall of Canada, Ltd., Toronto
Prentice-Hall of India Private Ltd., New Delhi
Prentice-Hall of Japan, Inc., Tokyo
Prentice-Hall of Southeast Asia Pte. Ltd., Singapore

10 9 8 7 6 5 4 3 2 1

Library of Congress Cataloging in Publication Data

Wahl, Jan.
        Dracula's cat.
        SUMMARY: A pet's eye view of life with Count Dracula.
1. Cats—Fiction.   2. Dracula—Fiction.
I. Chorao, Kay. II. Title.
PZ7. W1266 Dr   E   77-27051
ISBN 0-13-218933-X

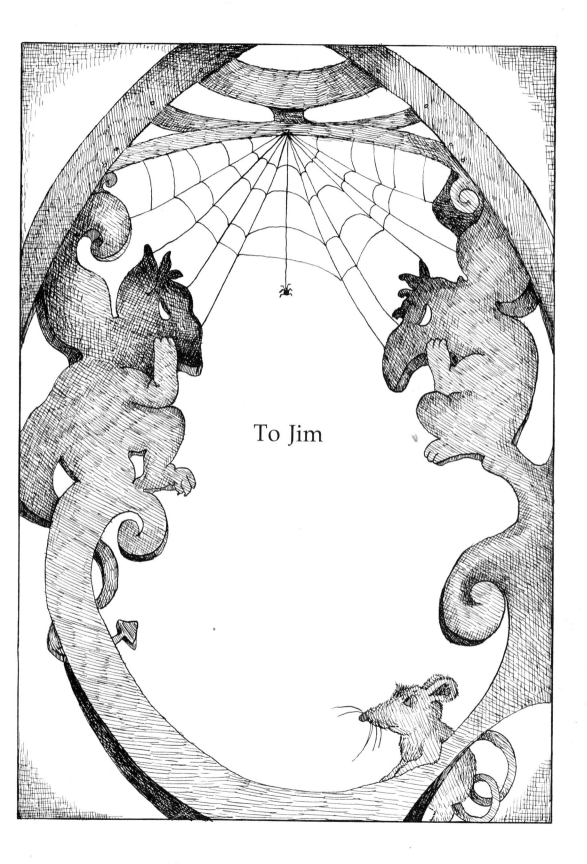

To Jim

This is the castle where my master Count Dracula lives. When the moon is full it's not *wise* to go there.

"Miaoow," I tell him. "Hey! It is time to wake up." Something howls in the woods. Dracula rises. Out of his coffin. He should get me my saucer of milk.

Tonight the moon is orange and big. He for-
gets my milk! With his cloak on he crawls like
a lizard down the wall. His carriage waits.
Well! I had better follow . . .

"MER-rowww!" I cry. *"I* want to come!" I jump fast. The carriage is pulled by coal-black horses into the night. Owls hoot. Dry leaves whistle in the wind. I snuggle close to him.

The carriage stops near Mistress Agatha's cottage. He is going to SCARE her. I see the look in his eyes. My master steps out. Walking as quiet as cobwebs!

Shh! He knocks at the door. I rub my face with my paw. Moonbeams twinkle. Dracula changes. *Into a wolf.* He growls. What a delicious spooky sound it is!

A tiny window opens. Mistress Agatha's head
pokes out. Now she cries: "Just wait a
minute, Old Dracula!" I try to warn him.
"Miaoooww!" Oh. Too late!

Mistress Agatha dumps a bucket of pig slop on him. He shudders and shakes. My master bays at the moon: "Woo-OO!" Once more changing shape. This time into—

the shape of a *bat!* Fluttering up. Up in air!
Beating his wings on the window. I hear loud
clatter of wood shoes running THUNK!
THUNK! downstairs. Red-faced Mistress
Agatha dashes forth. With a broom.

She yells, giving him a whack. "Take that, Old Dracula!" He flies off into the apple tree boughs. I follow.

My master, the bat, gets stuck in high tree
limbs. What can I do to help? I crawl up the
apple tree.

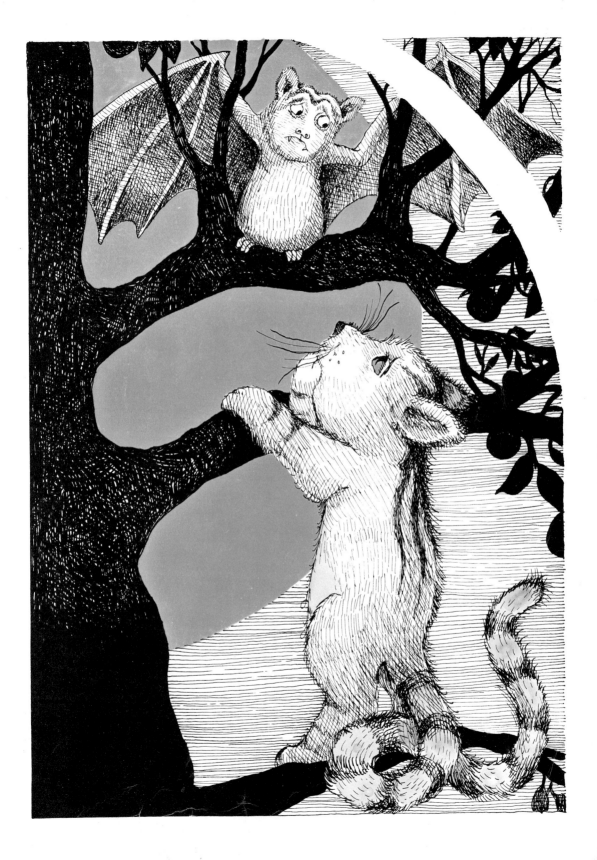

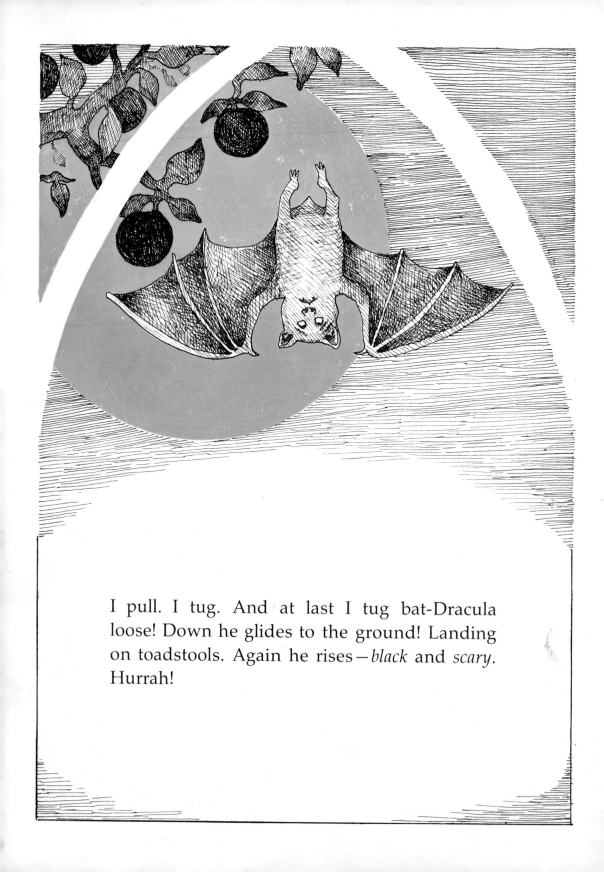

I pull. I tug. And at last I tug bat-Dracula loose! Down he glides to the ground! Landing on toadstools. Again he rises—*black* and *scary*. Hurrah!

In the rattling carriage, he holds me in his lap.
He tickles my whiskers. He strokes my fur. I
love it. I am carried back home. A candle is lit
in the kitchen.

He pours me a whole, huge pitcher of sweet milk. PURRR! IT'S SO COZY TO BE DRACULA'S OWN CAT!